Marisolandia

Marisolandia

Michelle Cruz Gonzales

wtaw press

Santa Rosa, CA

Library of Congress Cataloging-in-Publication data is on file with the Library of Congress.

ISBN: 979-8-9898729-1-6 (paperback)
ISBN: 979-8-9898729-2-3 (ebook)

WTAW Press
PO Box 2825
Santa Rosa, CA 95405
www.wtawpress.org

WTAW Press is a not-for-profit literary press. This publication is made possible by the generous contributions from individual donors, public arts organizations, and private foundations.

Para mi mamí, Cheryl Gonzales

La más chingona

"Catch me, as if I have surely been out
committing a violation against you,
my sin of insisting on existing without you."

—Ana Castillo

CombinationNation@combinationation.com
To: mmunguia@republic.com

Congratulations on your *Combination* and ensuring the Republic's goal of racial and ethnic harmony. You should be proud that you have taken your relationship with John Emery to the next level. Now that you've leveled up, it's important to remember that it's just as easy to stumble and fall.

Relationships need dedication and care. The more time you spend with your pareja, the closer you will become and the sooner you will be combined for life. Tentative coeds, click HERE for tips and suggestions. Love doves, click HERE for suggestions for your next getaway and discounts on vacation packages. Remember that using your courtesy government-issued device and engaging with Combination Nation's Program for Racial and Ethnic Harmony is your duty by law.

—

MARISOL WENT TO HER DRESSER and pulled out the black jeans she wore on the day she had sex with Moises. Losing her virginity with him had been her idea.

She took her device out of her purse. It was 4:00. If she was quick, she had time to shower, change, and find her way back to him.

She had showered in the morning, but her skin still crawled from John Emery's touch. After their Republic discounted weekend away at El Encanto Seahorse Inn, she had him drop her off at an rT stop near where she lived instead of in front of her building, saying she didn't want him to drive so far out of his way.

"Don't be silly." John rubbed her thigh. He was always rubbing her thigh.

"I can take my bag on the train. I did it on Friday."

It was their first weekend away after a few

dinner dates, and they left from work because she wanted to keep her work life separate from what little time she had of her own for as long as possible.

Combination Nation®, the Republic's de-facto social channel which flagrantly combined social media, hooking up, dating, marriage, shopping, entertainment, and "education" into one service, had sent Marisol alerts about John, and then one day he showed up at her desk to ask her out the old school way. He was Dean of Humanities, and that meant, in the Republic, he was the dean of fake music and the dean of fake art—basically, marketing designed to unify coeds. His first combination hadn't worked out, and he'd been by her desk a lot before they started "dating" to ask questions he could answer himself. Men had three extra years to make a combination, until the age of twenty-six, and Dean Emery had already been married and quickly divorced. It didn't look good for a twenty-eight-year-old in his line of work to be single. He was supposed to be a model post-secession Califorñio—and, according to Combination Nation®, her perfect match.

The day she registered for Combination Nation®, the results popped up on the screen: "Suitable match for tall, vanilla male professional." In theory, John Emery was a good combination for her because he was a few years older and he was local. But she was sure her relatively dark skin was the reason Combination Nation® suggested she combine with a vanilla guy. The dating service described her as medium spicy, and the app sent her frequent reminders to stay out of the sun.

"I already know where you live." John

turned to look her in the eye. He had one hand on the steering wheel even though he wasn't steering his made-to-order self-driving vehicle.

"I can look anything up on the campus intranet." He tapped on the wheel like he was tapping his computer screen with his free hand. "I have that level of access." He lifted his hand from her thigh.

She tugged the hem of her skirt back over her knee.

He laughed like he was making a joke, but she knew what he really meant about access. He had made that clear at the Seahorse Inn, and now what he did to her sounded in her head like an air-raid siren.

—

"I SAW THE WAY THAT piano player was looking at you." John said as he lowered himself onto one of the chairs by the window in their room. Marisol tried to think quickly about how to change the subject, for John was clearly drunk. She looked around the room, its fresh coat of paint, sturdy minimal furnishings and muted colors, the hallmarks of Republic branding. Though she'd had two glasses of wine, John ordered and finished most of a second bottle.

"You should drink some water," she said finally and went to the mini fridge at the other end of the room and got bottles for them. She opened one and handed it to him.

"Thank you." He set the bottle on the table in front of him.

"Tomatelo." She tilted her own bottle toward her mouth in case he didn't understand.

“Kiss me first,” he said, and he patted his knee.

“You said you could wait.” She took a sip of water.

“Did I?” He wobbled out of his chair and grabbed her by the wrist and pulled him to her. He buried his face in her chest and stuck one hand up the back of her dress. “Besame.” He pulled her even closer, one hand on her ass.

On the bed, Marisol didn’t want him getting on top and smothering her, so she straddled him and let him fondle her and grind into her. The zipper of his slacks dug into her thigh.

She’d told him she had only been with a few men because he’d expect at least a few. And she’d said she hadn’t had the time to get tested for a few months. He barely took the time to put on a condom before climbing on top of her and fucking her in a way that he evidently thought would make her want more, cupping her face with his hands and saying, "Qué bonita eres, tan sexy, tan bella," with a French accent because French was the language he'd studied in college. She didn't know if it was the wine or something else, but she felt afraid, sad, disgusted, and separate from her body all at the same time.

He'd worn a condom, but she used her diaphragm too. She couldn't bear the idea of his leche swimming around inside of her.

—

IN THE SHOWER, MARISOL TURNED the water on as hot as she could stand, and she used her loofa to scrub her arms, chest, hips and thighs until the skin was bright red. Scrubbing hard felt like the only way to remove John from her body. When she couldn't stand the stinging a second longer, she turned on the cold water and watched as any real, or imagined, John Emery DNA ran down the drain—waste into the sewer.

She toweled off, pulled on her black jeans and black tank top, and looked in the mirror. Except for the knot that felt like a fist in her gut, she was a whole different Marisol, not the Marisol who smoothed her skirt and wore a flower in her hair, the Marisol John saw. She liked the way the jeans looked, how unfussy they were compared to the clothes she wore to work, the pencil skirts and pussy bows. She had jeans before she met Moises but she rarely wore them. She liked the way they held her tight, like armor, a thick layer between prying eyes or hands.

The scrap of paper Moises had given her the night she'd given him her virginity was safe in her back pocket. Moises was contaminado, a Mexicano and a goatherd who she'd met only a few weeks before in her neighborhood. He was there with his flock of FPGs, fire prevention goats who grazed the dry land on the hills close to her apartment. He was one of those in the Republic who was invisible, in the background of real life, and she hadn't noticed him at first either, only the goats. They became friends just as Combination Nation® paired her with John.

To avoid being reported to Combination Nation®, she'd visited him inside the Pioneer Spirit, his goatherd RV, where he lived most of the year. He towed the RV along with the goats from one dry fire-prone neighborhood to the next. Inside, the trailer had everything a person might need in miniature: a kitchen, a table, a bathroom, and a bed.

They were sitting at the compact kitchen table, each on their built-in seat, Moises directly across from her. She could feel the heat from his legs near hers and hear the occasional bleating of goats. She wanted to stay there forever.

"There's something I should tell you." Moises reached out and grabbed Marisol's hand.

She'd never felt his skin on hers, she hadn't even allowed the idea to enter her head. As far as the Republic was concerned, Moises was nobody, a shadowy figure, necessary hands for work that couldn't be done through machine learning.

"Antes que anything happens here"—he

gestured toward his heart and then hers—"that isn't *supposed to*, I need you to know something about me." He squeezed her hand.

Marisol felt all the air go out of her, but she kept her hand in his.

"I'm in a group, not like a pandilla, or a gang, but it's a group, like a band but more than that, chingao." He pulled his hand away.

Marisol leaned back. "A band? Like music?"

"Sí, dangerous music, underground." He lowered his voice. "Like actual resistance music."

"I don't get it. I thought you were just—" She pressed her lips together and stopped.

"Just a goatherd, un cabrero." He looked away toward the window.

Marisol turned and listened for the bleating of goats, then she turned and looked at

Moises. "I've been assigned to someone at work. It's all been arranged." She covered Moises's hand with both of her hands.

"I'll be gone all weekend."

His face went blank.

She stood and shoved her hands in her back pockets.

Anger, worry, disgust, she wasn't sure what he was feeling. They had only just begun doing whatever this was. She was just visiting the goats when he had first invited her in for some jamaica, a hibiscus drink she could never resist.

"You mean next weekend?" he said.

"Yes, and"—she swallowed hard—"I'm a virgin. Una cereza?"

"Cereza? That's made up," he said.

"That I'm a virgin?"

"No, esa palabra." He tapped the table.

"That's a Republic thing. In Spanish, una cereza is just fruit."

Marisol's cheeks burned. Now I look like a cherry, she thought. She looked down to avoid his stare, willed him to understand why she was there, and said, "It's just …"

He stood up and faced her, softening. "You don't want him to have it."

Marisol shook her head and stepped in close. She took one of his hands, squeezed it, and then slid it under her top. "Me, I don't want him to have me."

MARISOL LOOKED INTO THE MIRROR one more time, at the tank top and jeans and the way the shower and the clothes had transformed her appearance. She unfolded the scrap of paper Moises had slid into her pocket, the hand-drawn map of his new location, another several acres of dry grass further away. She pushed away her worry that she wouldn't find him, that he'd be gone, or worse, that he didn't—as the Republic would have it—really exist at all.

She tied her ash gray hoodie around her waist and looked again at her device. The photos John had posted on Combination Nation® of them together had posted automatically to her page, and she had to "like" them all, tap, tap, tap, tap. She'd heard stories about what might have happened to people who hadn't complied and followed the system, but no one really knew where they'd gone once their accounts were deleted. She tossed the device on the bed.

She studied the map a last time before tucking it back into her pocket and slipping out the door. She walked around the backside of the building to avoid her best friend, Colleen, from seeing her through the kitchen window. No doubt Colleen was there soaking beans for Mexican food Monday.

She took the rT for two stops before getting onto a city bus. Barely aware of the shops on the main avenue sliding by, her mind went over a story she'd been following about Charles Rifkin, the former born-and-raised Califorño who had written *Relocation Nation*, a memoir about the expulsion and forced relocation of Blacks. People outside of the Republic were writing about what was going on here, articles she accessed in all sorts of shady ways. The article covered an event in the book where Rifkin told the story of the police stopping him on his way home from his job as an air-traffic controller in Sacramento, taking him to an unmarked detention center for processing, loading him onto a bus, and sending him out of the state. Weeks later, when his family members were eventually notified, they were told they would never learn his whereabouts unless they left the state to join him, and they were forced to give up their property and assets in the process. Later, Rifkin was accused of "biting the hand that feeds him" for criticizing Arizona's increased, disproportionate police shootings of Black and Brown people: "The same impulse to shoot Black and Brown citizens of Arizona in the back is the very same impulse that inspired our expulsion from the Republic."

From the bus stop, she walked until she

got to the hill drawn on the map—at least she hoped it was the hill on the map. She couldn't check her device because she had left it behind to avoid being tracked. But she was so used to having it on her that she now got phantom notifications as she walked, felt random buzzing in her back pocket. She knew when she got home, she'd have multiple notifications from John and Combination Nation® urging her to post again or plan another weekend getaway. After a half-mile climb, Marisol thought she saw the roof of the trailer peeking through the branches from a grove of bay trees. After several more yards, she heard the dogs. Soon enough they were at her side. Then the trailer door swung open. It was Moises, his head freshly shaved.

"You're here." He hugged her and pulled her toward the trailer.

Marisol stiffened but followed along.

"Are you okay?" he asked once he'd shut the door.

"Tired." She swallowed hard and choked back the lump in her throat she'd tried to push down the whole day.

"Do you want to talk about it?"

She shook her head and sat at the table.

Moises filled a glass with water and ice and set it on the table before her. Avoiding her eyes, he said, "We all do shit we don't want to do to save our own necks."

She hoped Moises had never had to let someone he could barely stand to even think about take off his clothes and violate him. She adjusted the sweatshirt around her waist, pulling the sleeves closer.

"I'd still like to cortar his dick off," Moises said.

"No lo quiero hablar." Her voice cracked. She took a sip of water.

"Ok, lo siento." He knelt in front of her and squeezed her knee. "Are you ready to meet the band? Los Fugitivx Desparecidx?" His voice was soft.

Marisol dabbed at the corner of her eyes with the knuckle of each forefinger. "Should I wear lipstick?"

"You should wear whatever makes you comfortable." He stood and held out his hand.

"But you told me to wear black, no?"

"I just didn't want you to feel out of place at the show."

Marisol stood. "Pareces bien firme, así."

"Firme?"

"Si, firme."

When Moises opened the trailer door, the sun was low on the horizon. "Lista?"

She was ready. Ready to leave what had happened at the Seahorse Inn behind her.

"Orale, or we're going to be too late." He went out the door.

Marisol walked faster to keep up with Moises and reached out and grabbed his hand.

On the way down the hill, Moises prepared Marisol to meet the band.

"I can't use my real name in the band. I go by Meztli."

"What does it mean?"

"It's Nahua. All our band names are Nahua. Meztli, significa luna, Marisol."

Marisol turned quick to face him. "Moon, de veras?"

"Si, de veras."

Her name, Marisol, meant ocean and sun.

He stopped, took her hand, and traced the shape of a crescent moon on her palm. He continued, "Our guitar player is Xochilt or Xochi, the bass player is Cualli, and Atl is the drummer.

Marisol looked at Moises. "Atl?"

"It means water, like fluid. They use neutral pronouns."

The Republic had several regional community living centers like the one she lived in, but Marisol didn't know anybody who lived in one of the trans centers.

At the bottom of the hill, an unmarked, windowless white van was parked behind a grove of trees that separated the highway from the dirt road. The band members waited for them inside. Atl opened the side door to let them in. Xochi sat in the driver's seat and Cualli rode shotgun. They were all beautiful, boxy and muscular and flat-chested, with wide high-arched natural eyebrows, short hair, and eyeliner. They were stunning. Marisol's chest tightened again. It felt like time travel from the weekend with John, her feelings still raw, but she didn't know in which direction—a future better time, or maybe a time like before the secession.

Atl shook Marisol's hand. "Mucho gusto, Marisol. Lista para cantar con nosotrx?"

Zas! Something electric tingled, from Marisol's fingers up her arm and through her chest, some familiar current of energy. Something deep within her loosened. She had understood what they'd said when for so long she had thought nearly all her Spanish was lost. But like many things perdido, things stolen, some memory remained. Yes, she was ready to sing with them.

"Mucho gusto," she said, her eyes blurry with tears. Moises put his hand on her back, but she moved away and covered her face. She was not going to fall apart.

She could feel everyone watching her, and she heard the engine of the van shut off.

"What's wrong?" Xochi had climbed out of the driver's seat and was walking toward Marisol and Moises.

Marisol shook her head, swallowed hard. This was not how she wanted them to know her, a wreck of a girl from the Republic, a girl on the arm of the singer of their band.

Xochi stood before her. "Marisol, I feel like putting my hand on your shoulder. Is that okay?"

Marisol nodded, and Xochi reached out and put a firm hand on Marisol's shoulder.

Everyone watched until Moises broke the silence. "Xochi isn't just the guitar player," he said. "She's the leader of the band, como la mama."

"Eh, I'm not your mom, cabrón, just la mama of the band."

Now the whole band was standing around Marisol in a circle. She again felt the current of energy rippling all around her.

Xochi put her hand out toward Marisol. "Una limpia could help."

Marisol looked at Moises.

"A cleansing," he clarified and nodded in agreement with Xochi.

"Si, una limpia, primero, with your consent of course, Marisol."

Marisol was familiar with curanderismo, but she had never had a limpia. When she felt off, she put a clean glass of water under her bed to ward off negative energy, something she had learned from her own mom. Starting in kindergarten, Marisol started having bad dreams even sometimes when she slept in bed with her parents. While her dad soothed her, her mom would go to the kitchen to get one glass of water for Marisol to drink and another to put under the bed.

Xochi opened the passenger-side door and pulled a drawstring bag out of the glove box. "Meztli, Cualli, stay in the van."

Xochi led the way to a thicket of trees. Marisol followed, and Atl trailed behind them both.

"No tengas miedo," Xochi said to Marisol when they stopped. "Moises told me where you've been."

Marisol's cheeks burned.

Atl shuffled their feet. "Don't worry, he didn't tell everyone. He didn't tell me."

Xochi took a simple black cup, a copalero,

out of the drawstring bag and handed it to Atl while she took some copal from another smaller bag. She placed the copal into the copalero and lit it with a match.

Marisol stood with her hands at her sides. She didn't know what else to do. She just hoped this would help her to never think of John—*nunca jamas,* ever again. Her mamá would have said it biting down hard on the h sound of the Arabic J.

The copal sent up smoke as Xochi knelt at Marisol's feet. She passed the copalero around Marisol's ankles, up her legs, and slowed at her hips, passing it several times around her pelvis, before drawing it up to her chest, around her heart and then around her head. Marisol breathed in the smoke circling her head and exhaled in a long sigh. She understood that it wasn't so much the smoke but the care the others were taking of her.

Xochi passed the copalero to Atl, who walked with it around them both as they spoke, Atl repeating each phrase after Xochil.

"El cuerpo tuyo es el cuerpo tuyo, no es de nadie más. La mente tuyo, es el mente tuya, no es de nadie más, y nadie la va a robar."

Xochi touched her hand to her own chest and said, "Your body," and then she touched her hand to her head and said, "your mind, and nobody can take that away."

Marisol nodded and closed her eyes. Tears streamed down her cheeks. She didn't wipe them away.

A breeze rustled the dry branches. Marisol opened her eyes. Xochi and Atl stood waiting in front of her.

"Abrazo?" Atl held out their arms.

Marisol stepped forward to let Atl wrap their strong arms around her in a tight hug. Xochi knelt and rummaged in the leaves, found a rock, and extinguished the copal inside the copalero.

When they returned to the van, Moises opened the door to let her and Atl into the backseat.

"Como te sientes?" He took Marisol's hand and squeezed it.

Marisol nodded. The tightness in her chest had given way.

"We want you to be here with us esta noche, to leave all that behind."

ON THE RIDE TO the warehouse where Fugitivx

would play, Marisol sat between Moises and Atl. They both smelled freshly showered but still earthy and real. Moises leaned his leg into hers as they drove. Marisol was glad he didn't try to put his arm around her like she was his property.

As the van zipped along the freeway, Marisol learned that Cualli had wanted the band to have a Nahua name, Mitotiqui, which meant disturbance, but in the end, they decided it sounded too much like the name of a world music group—that fake music genre that was just music people in The Republic found palatable. People would get a better idea of what the band was about if they were called X Fugitivx Desparecidx in Spanish because it didn't need translation.

Marisol had only ever read about the neighborhood where the warehouse stood.

The rT didn't stop there. Full of abandoned lots and factories, the neighborhood was adjacent to a part of the city that super-developers didn't want to touch because it was still contaminated by underground chemical spills from around the time of the secession. The Republic kept the streets clean through frequent sweeps of the homeless encampments, an effort to maintain the illusion of Republic-as-provider, but the facades of most buildings appeared to be crumbling in disrepair.

Before getting out of the van, the band members painted their faces with heavy black and red costume paint. Moises and Xochi each painted wide black bands over the bridges of their noses and their eyes and white dots down their cheeks. Atl and Cualli had red bands with black dots.

"These aren't authentic designs." Xochi

passed around the bag for everyone to put their makeup back into. "It's just a disguise, since we can't sing with masks on to avoid surveillance."

Moises looked at Marisol. "People aren't supposed to take photos when we play, but we can't take any chances."

Punk music was blasting through the sound system when they entered the warehouse. The building doubled as an occasional underground club. It had graffitied, tangerine-colored walls and high ceilings lined with tattered tissue paper papel picado and fabric bunting with the names of what Marisol thought must be other bands spray painted on them: Ausencia, Trap Girl, El Condenado, and Los Crudos. The papel picado of dancing skull cutouts reminded Marisol of what she'd learned in an art history class about the Mexican Revolution. Certain ethnic groups, like the Chinese, were not welcomed by the Revolutionaries. The professor, Señora Flores, was a Mexicana who sat amongst the students in a circle of chairs they'd drawn together for their discussion. Her long black hair was piled high on her head and bobbed as she spoke. "Of course, expelling any one group is never ideal, but one must appreciate the vulnerable position Mexíco was in at the time in the development of its national character." A student raised his hand. He was the only other Mexicano in the class beside Marisol. She hoped he'd say something about how her interpretation of the expulsion of Chinese from Mexico sounded a lot like recent expulsions done in the name of the Republic. The teacher nodded at the young man, a sign that it was his turn to speak.

"I know this happened a long time ago," he said, "before widespread awareness about who we all are and where we came from, but Mexican officials have always known that Mexicans are already a mixed-race people."

Señora Flores nodded. "Fair point, but race and culture are two very different matters. What we are discussing in this class is art and culture. That is our focus today." A year or so later, when Marisol took a job with the college, she noticed the class was no longer offered and searched the meeting minutes to learn it had been axed due to budget cuts. The minutes reported that a now-retired dean had declared the course unnecessary for citizens of the Republic.

A low stage stretched out at one end of the warehouse. It was loaded with amps, a drum kit, and several other drums—congas, a cajon, and a large Mexica drum, the kind used in Aztec dance ceremonies still common in the

Republic. The room filled with people of all different ages. There were a few combined co-eds and several Mexicano couples. It had never occurred to Marisol that happily combined co-eds would disagree so much with the Republic that they would take the risk of coming all this way to see a band whose whole message lay in direct opposition. Some wore black jean vests with studs, buttons with band names on them, including Fugitivx. She saw several hand-painted Fugitivx Desparecidx jackets too. The majority of the crowd were Mexicanos, other goatherds, gardeners, field hands. Most combined coeds wore regular clothes, and as Moises had suggested, stood out a little, but no one seemed to care—just being there made you clandestine. People who dressed up too much at shows were assumed to be informants.

Moises, Xochil, Cualli, and Atl set their

guitars on the stage. Atl was to use the drum set on the stage, backline, they called it—they brought their own snare drum and cymbals. In the van Moises mentioned they were the only band playing, and since there were no permits for these shows, they were sometimes broken up by la chota. He had tried to be reassuring, but then he said if the cops did show up, for Marisol to pull her hoodie down over her eyes as far as she could and to run straight for the van, which they always left open just in case.

Marisol spotted a young Mexicano couple, jovencitos, standing by the stage and holding hands, no more than sixteen. The boy looked distinctly Mexicano to her, but he was light-skinned. The girl he was with had long black hair and brown skin like hers. They kissed, leaning against a speaker. At their age, they were not yet required to register on

Combination Nation®, but they were supposed to be practicing coeds. This was certainly the only place they could be together like this, just as it was for her and Moises. She hoped they knew how to avoid being tracked and had left their devices at home.

Moises came up behind her. "They met here." He squeezed her hand.

"I have never seen a couple like that before," she said. She couldn't help but stare, even as they kissed, the young man's hand on his girlfriend's waist.

"Never?" He pointed at himself and then her.

She pushed his finger away. "We're not a couple."

"They are Mara and Naveen, children of coeds. I met them at our last show." Moises put his hand on Marisol's back and whispered in her ear, "Not acting like hermanos at all."

"One white parent and one Mexicano?" Technically, a couple like that could do whatever they wanted, but she knew it wouldn't be allowed. The Combination Nation® algorithm would never suggest them as a match.

"This so-called combining thing isn't as clear-cut as the Republic expected."

Marisol knew what he meant. It was not a real secret that the Republic hoped to create people who were ethnically ambiguous, not light-skinned and not dark-skinned. The ideal was people with tans who had blue or green eyes, hardy and beautiful, but not appearing as dark-skinned or particularly indigenous. They were like the people who Marisol had seen in fashion magazines and ads before the secession, beautifully muted people whose ethnicity didn't call up fears or stereotypes.

The warehouse space had nearly filled by the time the Fugitivx had set up to play. Everyone watched the stage, eager to see the band play their music, deliver their message. No one was drinking alcohol or smoking, like Marisol had expected. There was a courtyard with a barbeque grill, and food and water was handed out to anyone who wanted or needed it.

The band had waited for the sun to go down and the crescent moon to rise high in the sky before playing to make it easier for people to leave quickly in the dark if the show was shut down. A ceiling projector that Marisol hadn't noticed filled the wall behind the stage with scenes from what used to be the US/Mexico border before it was moved back—drone camera footage of miles and miles of border wall, a wide shot of the wall extending even a quarter mile into the ocean. At the beach front, the camera dropped down along the Mexican side of the fence where people had graffitied messages. "Aqui rebotan todos los sueños," "Everything is under control," "Caution ICE ahead," "Which way to freedom?" with arrows pointing in all directions. The drone picked up speed, and the fencing of the wall blurred as it neared the water and then lifted out over the waves. Moises stayed at her side while Marisol watched, caught up in the video, then suddenly Xochi's guitar went off, sounding like an engine revving at the speed of the drone over the ocean blue. Atl shouted, "Un-dos-tres," and Moises launched from Marisol's side straight onto the stage and sang.

Se pueden ir, pero se quieren quedar

They can go,
but they stay anyway

Moises sang in Spanish and Xochi came in just behind him, singing in English. It was the song Marisol knew, "Calicaca," the one song that Moises played for her through his device.

No hay eleccion propio/
solamente cadenas sin llave

No choices, just fake ones,
and locks without a key

After the first explosive song, Moises sounded out of breath. He half sang and half spoke, "We're all here esta noche para resistir our mental, economic, and regional imprisonment." He leaned from the stage and handed

Marisol a stack of pamphlets with the band's lyrics printed on them.

"Start at the back." He began passing out the pamphlets to those in front of the stage.

Marisol went to the back of the room and gave a booklet to anyone with outstretched hands.

"If you came with someone, please share," Xochi said into her microphone.

Atl began a steady low rumbling drum-beat. Their drum grew louder as Moises and Marisol finished with the pamphlets.

On stage Moises said into the mic, "This is called 'Strangulation Nation,'" and Xochi's guitar came in loud and fast with Moises's vocals, and she sang on the chorus. The crowd sang along too, undulating forward and back, fists in the air. Some people simply danced, singing to themselves along the edge of the stage.

Back at the front of the stage, Marisol watched Moises transformed from goatherd to singer, conductor of energy and anger. The muscles in his neck strained against his skin as he screamed each palabra, sweat beaded at his brow. It was like nothing she'd seen before. He was not exotic, or suave, or caliente. He was nothing like the piano player who had snuck illicit glances at her at the restaurant with John Emery. He was the opposite of all that, his anger so vivid and palpable that white women and white men too would be terrified—and with reason.

The young Mexicano couple, Mara and Naveen, danced and sang each word. Moises lowered the microphone to let them hear their own voices soar through the room.

After two more songs, with the crowd singing along, and a break in between, Moises helped Atl fix something on the drum set and announced they had a new song. Marisol read the lyrics on the pamphlet.

"La se llama, 'Nuevo Gringolandia.' It's about all we've lost: our culture, our language, our parents. It's about being put into orphanages and reprogrammed."

Marisol swallowed hard.

"If you're old enough, close your eyes and try to remember your life the way it was before. Picture someone you loved, someone who loved you—tu mamá, tu papá, una tía, tu abuelita. De donde tiraron a mi abuelita?"

Marisol kept her eyes fixed on Moises, hoping not to cry there at the head of the stage. She held her breath. She understood. *Where did they throw my grandma?*

"De don—de tira—ron a mi abuelita?" He

said again and wiped at his eyes with the back of his hand.

"Un-dos-tres." Atl counted and clicked their sticks together, and the band launched into "Nuevo Gringolandia," playing it amplified and live for the first time, Moises and Xochi singing together. Xochi's voice was higher and she sang fast in English, the pitch of her voice cutting over the top of Moises's baritone.

Nos quitaron todo y nos
llenaron con verguenza
Nos quitaron todo y nos
llenaron con mentiras

They filled us with lies
They filled us with shame

Nos quitaron la lengua
nos quitaron todo

They stole our tongue
They took everything

Nos quitaron todo y nos
llenaron con mentiras
Nos quitaron todo y nos
llenaron con deber
Nos quitaron todo y nos
llenaron con gringolandia

There was a brief instrumental break and Xochi stepped forward and played a short guitar solo. At the end of the solo, Moises shouted at the crowd. "Otra vez, todos juntos. Everyone together!"

Marisol joined in, mouthing, singing, shouting the words.

When Moises announced their last song, Xochi invited anyone who wanted to join them on stage. The song was "Curiosidad," a Crudos song, a Latinx punk band from the

1990s Xochi had told her about in the van. Marisol stayed close to the stage, while twenty-five or so young people jumped in, some crowded around the microphone stands and others taking a place behind one of the extra drums. The song opened with guitar feedback and a screechy sound pattern, and it lasted a total of fifty seconds.

Moises wound his fist in the air, "Una vez mas!"

Xochi repeated the guitar intro and different people jumped on stage to get a turn at the two microphones. Moises ended the song by repeating the line, "Busca la verdad, busca la verdad, busca la verdad, busca la verdad."

Find the truth.

—

www.Seenit.com/FugitiveCalifornio/NewMexico

A fugitive Californio is reported to have been transported from The Republic of California to New Mexico by members of the band Fugitivx Desparecidx (The Fugitive Disappeared, all genders). While punk rock music and its related subculture movements gained ground in California, Republic leaders believe that rebellious self-expression through fashion, and indeed punk rock itself, is no longer necessary because cultural values and traditions are respected and have replaced the need for sub-cultures or social movements. Some contend that punk rock culture is largely superficial, expressed as fashion through use of the color black, leather jackets, spikes, animal print, and torn or distressed fabrics. Officials were contacted for this story, but none were available for comment.

To date, very few cases of successful defection from the Republic have been confirmed, even though defections have been reported in each of the bordering states. The fugitive Californio, whose name has not been released to ensure their protection, was met by relatives in Las Cruces, New Mexico. A distant relative of the fugitive Californio, one source for this story, also not named, reported that the members of Los Fugitivx Desparecidx sing in Spanish and claim to be escaped Californios. Reportedly based somewhere in New Mexico, the band has no website and no social media accounts and could not be reached for comment.

ABOUT THE AUTHOR

PUNK WRITER, MICHELLE CRUZ GONZALES was born in Los Angeles, the second largest Mexican city in the world, and she writes about the intersections between race, class, and gender. During the 1990s, Gonzales cut her writing teeth as a lyricist and drummer in the all-woman hardcore punk band Spitboy. Gonzales and the band are featured in the movie *Turn It Around: Story of East Bay Punk.* Her memoir *The Spitboy Rule: Tales of a Xicana in a Female Punk Band* (PM Press) documents her experiences traveling with Spitboy as the drummer, one of the primary lyricists, and the one woman of color. She has published in literary journals such as *The Los Angeles Review of Books*, anthologies, including *Listen To Your Mother: What They Said Then, What They're Saying Now* (Penguin Random House), and online publications such as Latino Rebels, Longreads, Razorcake, and Alta Journal. Gonzales holds an MFA in English/Creative Writing from Mills College where she minored in ethnic studies. She has been on the English faculty at Las Positas College since 2005, has two dogs, Pawblo and Pedro, and one son, Luis Manuel. She lives with her marido, J.Inés, in Oakland, California.

ACKNOWLEDGMENTS

WRITING A NOVEL AND MAKING a longer work stand alone is not something I could have done without my trusted readers, namely Jenny Forrester. Early readers of this world are Karin Spirn, Ariel Gore, Tomás Moniz, and Ivy Clift. Mi marido, Inés Peralta Hernández, read the whole longer work too, and is my Mexican Spanish advisor. For all the haters, Mexican Spanish is a whole thing of its own, a legit language containing multiple other languages and words from indigenous Mexican languages. Don't get me started on Spanglish—chalé! Did you see the artwork by Sofía Belen Criswell? Thank you, Sofía, for painting on a deadline and creating something drawn from my work. I'll thank my hijo here too, Luis Manuel Gonzales Peralta, for introducing me to Sofía in the first place. *Marisolandia* would not exist if not for the support and encouragement of Peg Alford Pursell and Why There Are Words Press. Finally, dejame thank Peg Alford Pursell, otra vez, and Roxanne Guiney for their editorial contributions, the way they listened and pushed me to bring Marisol even more into the light.

ABOUT WTAW PRESS

WTAW PRESS IS A 501(C)(3) nonprofit publisher devoted to discovering and publishing enduring literary works of prose. WTAW publishes and champions a carefully curated list of titles across a range of genres (literary fiction, creative nonfiction, and prose that falls somewhere in between), subject matter, and perspectives.

WTAW Press Alcove Chapbook Series publishes chapbooks of prose selected through an annual competition. The competition is open to new, emerging, and established writers. We encourage writers of traditionally underrepresented and marginalized communities and first-time authors to send their work.

As a nonprofit literary press, WTAW depends on the support of donors. We are grateful for the assistance we receive from organizations, foundations, and individuals. WTAW Press especially wishes to thank the following individuals for their sustained support.

To find out more about our mission and publishing programs, or to make a donation, please visit wtawpress.org.

OTHER TITLES AVAILABLE FROM THE WTAW PRESS ALCOVE CHAPBOOK SERIES

Promiscuous Ruins by Julian Mithra,
Winner of the First Annual Alcove Prize

Eggs in Purgatory by Genanne Walsh

Mississippi River Museum
by Keith Pilapil Lesmeister

Something I Might Say by Stephanie Austin

Outtakes by Joanna Acevedo

Sarra Copia: A Locked-in Life
by Nancy Ludmerer

The Haunt by Liz Green,
Winner of the Second Annual Alcove Prize